An I Can Read Book®

W9-BTT-079

BUZBY

by JULIA HOBAN

Pictures by John Himmelman

HarperTrophy®
A Division of HarperCollins*Publishers*

HarperCollins®, 🖌®, Harper Trophy®, and I Can Read Book®
are trademarks of HarperCollins Publishers Inc.
BUZBY
Text copyright © 1990 by Julia Hoban
Illustrations copyright © 1990 by John Himmelman
Manufactured in China. All rights reserved.
For information address HarperCollins Children's Books,
a division of HarperCollins Publishers, 195 Broadway,
New York, NY 10007.
www.harpercollinschildrens.com

Library of Congress Cataloging-in-Publication Data
Hoban, Julia.
  Buzby / by Julia Hoban ; illustrated by John Himmelman.
    p.   cm.—(An I can read book)
  Summary: Buzby the cat takes a job at a hotel as a busboy
and creates all kinds of havoc before he ends up in a special job
created just for him.
  ISBN 0-06-022399-5.—ISBN 0-06-022398-7 (lib. bdg.)
  ISBN 0-06-444152-0 (pbk.)
  [1. Cats—Fiction. 2. Work—Fiction. 3. Hotels, motels, etc.—
Fiction.] I. Himmelman, John, ill. II. Title. III. Series.
PZ7.H63487Bu   1990   89-29408
[E]—dc20   CIP
                                                                  AC

First Harper Trophy edition, 1992.

19 20 SCP 30 29 28 27 26

For Benjamin Bunny-Bun

One day Mrs. Cat said,

"Buzby, you are a big kitten now.

It is time for you to get a job."

Buzby twitched his whiskers.

"I know how to lie in the sun,"

he said.

"I know how to nap in the grass.

I know how to catch mice.

But I do not know how to get a job."

"Buzby," said Mrs. Cat,

"you can get a job.

You are clean.

You are polite.

And you are a good mouser.

Now off you go."

Buzby walked down the road.

He came to Maple Leaf Farm.

There was a sign on the gate.

It said:

"That's me!" said Buzby.

"I have come for the job,"

he said to Farmer Brown.

"Are you a good mouser?"

asked Farmer Brown.

"I am a very good mouser,"

said Buzby.

Just then a big dog

came out of the barn

and growled.

"But I am sure you will find
another good mouser,"
said Buzby.
And he walked away quickly.

He came to Buttercup Dairy.

There was a sign on the fence.

It said:

"That's me!" said Buzby.

"I am very clean!"

"Step aside, sonny,"

said a big gray cat.

"There is room

for only one cat here,

and it is going to be me!"

15

"I did not want that job anyway,"

said Buzby,

and he walked on.

Buzby came to a town.

He saw a big hotel.

There was a sign outside the hotel.

It said:

"That's me!" said Buzby.

"They did not spell my name right,
but they know I am polite!"

"I am your man," Buzby said

to the hotel manager.

"You look more like a cat to me,"

said the manager.

"We need a busboy."

"A Buzby can be a busboy,"

said Buzby.

"A busboy is important,"

said the manager.

"He works in the dining room.

He has to fill all the glasses

with ice water.

He has to clear

all the dishes

and empty the ashtrays."

"I can do all of that,"

said Buzby.

"Are you polite?"

asked the manager.

"Sir," said Buzby,

"I am very polite."

"Well," said the manager,

"I guess we can give you a try."

Buzby walked through the hotel.

There were bellboys

in blue uniforms.

There were maids in white aprons.

"I am going to like working here,"

said Buzby.

He went into the kitchen.

"I am your new busboy,"

Buzby said to the cook.

"I have never had a cat
for a busboy," said the cook.
"Are your paws clean?"
"Very clean, sir," said Buzby.

"Then you are ready to start," said the cook.

He gave Buzby a white jacket with brass buttons.

"Remember," he said,

"we have some very important guests.

King Oswald is here.

He is sad,

because he lost his throne.

Be nice to him.

29

"We have Cecilia Hytone,

the opera singer,"

said the cook.

"No one has heard her sing in years,

but she is still famous.

Be polite to her."

"I am always polite," said Buzby.

"All right," said the cook.

"Your first job is to pour water
into all the glasses.

After that
you can clear the dishes."

"Yes, sir," said Buzby,
and he bowed politely.

Buzby went into the dining room.

There were flowers all around.

There were pink tablecloths

on every table.

Three parrots were sitting

at the first table.

Buzby poured water

into the first glass.

He was careful

and did not spill a drop.

Buzby poured water

into the second glass.

He was very careful

and did not spill a drop.

Buzby started to pour water
into the third glass.

"I should bow very low
to be extra polite,
because she is a lady,"
said Buzby to himself.

Buzby bowed very low.

SPLASH!

The ice water spilled
all over the lady's dress.

"*Laaaaah!*" she cried.

"*Do re mi fa so laaah!*"
she trilled.

"Madam, I am very sorry,"

said Buzby.

"*SO...RRY!*" sang the lady.

"*SO...SO...SO...SO...SORRY!*

I can sing again!

Thank you, thank you!"

She hugged Buzby.

Everyone clapped.

"Well," said Buzby,

"I think it is time

to clear the dishes."

Buzby looked around.

A walrus was sitting by himself.

He looked lonely.

"I will clear his dishes,"

said Buzby to himself.

He jumped on the table.

"Gadzooks!" cried the walrus.

"There is a cat on my table!"

"At your service, sir,"

said Buzby.

He bowed politely

and started to lick

the plates clean.

"Don't they feed you

in the kitchen?" asked the walrus.

"I am not hungry," said Buzby.

"I am your busboy.

I have to clear your dishes."

The walrus started to laugh.

"I have had lots of servants,"

said the walrus,

"but I have never had

a busboy like you."

Then he laughed some more.

"HO! HO! HO! HA! HA! HA!"

He laughed so hard

that all the other guests

started to laugh too.

"I am sorry, sir," said Buzby.

"Don't be sorry," said the walrus.

"I am King Oswald.

I have not laughed this much

since I lost my throne."

48

Buzby started

to get off the table,

but he slipped.

His hind paws

landed in the butter.

He tried to stand up,

but his paws were too slippery.

He spun around and around.

"A dancing cat!" cried King Oswald.

"What fun!"

Buzby's tail knocked over
the vase of flowers.

"KERCHOO!"

Buzby skidded

and somersaulted off the table.

CRASH!

"This is better than the circus!"

cried King Oswald.

Everyone cheered, "Yay! Yay!"

SLAM!

The kitchen doors opened,

and the cook came running out.

BANG!

The dining room doors opened,

and the manager came running in.

"What is going on?"

shouted the manager.

"I am very sorry, sir," said Buzby.

"Well," said the manager,

"I guess a Buzby

is not a busboy.

You are fired!"

Buzby stood up.

He took off his jacket.

He walked slowly to the door.

"Oh, no!" cried Cecilia Hytone.

"Buzby must stay!"

"Yes," said King Oswald,

"Buzby must stay!

If Buzby leaves,

then I will leave!"

"Wait, Buzby," said the manager.

"You may not be a good busboy,

but you make our guests happy.

I think there is a job for you

in this hotel after all."

"Sir," said Buzby,

"what job is that?"

"You can be our hotel cat!"

said the manager.

"Follow me.

I will show you what to do."

So Buzby got his own uniform,
and from then on
he stood at the door of the hotel
and looked after all the guests.

When his mother came to visit,

she said,

"See, Buzby, I told you

you could get a job.

"You are the best hotel cat

in the whole world!"

And he was!